I Went to the Beach

by Lori Morgan
pictures by Susan Kathleen Hartung

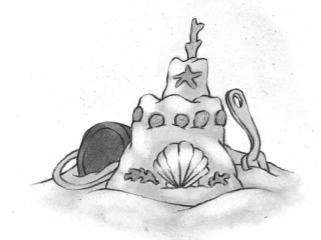

 Richard C. Owen Publishers, Inc.
Katonah, New York

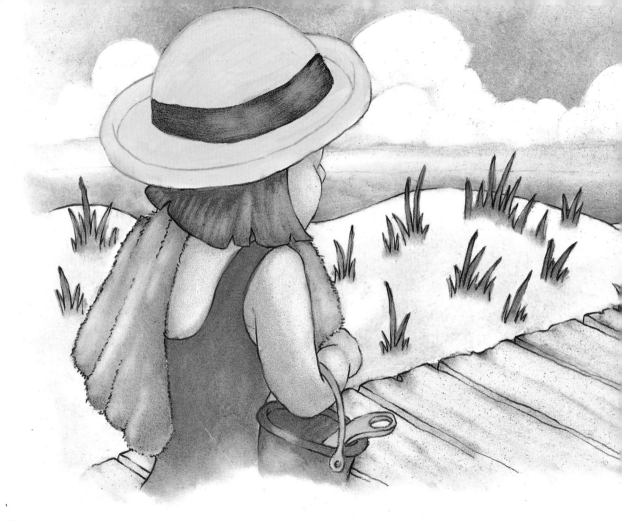

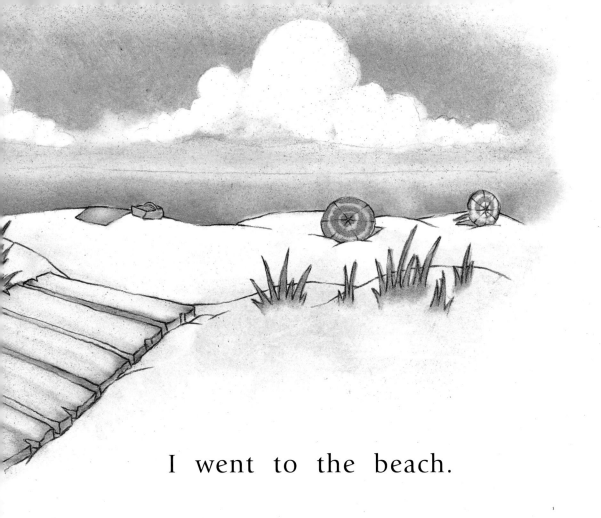

I went to the beach.

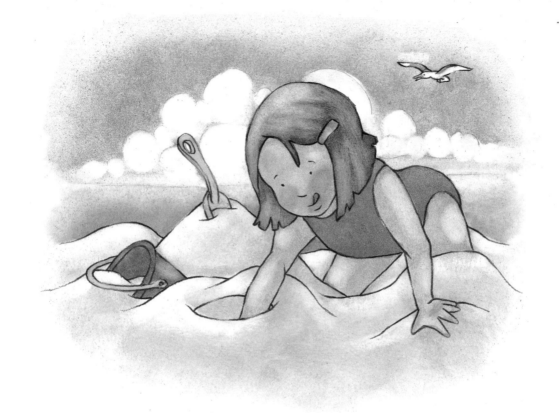

I dug a hole.

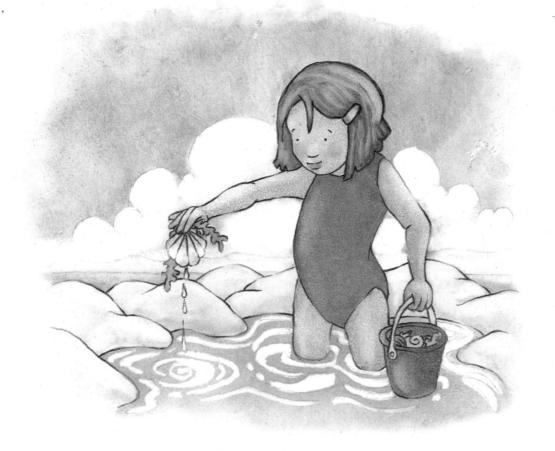

I found a shell.

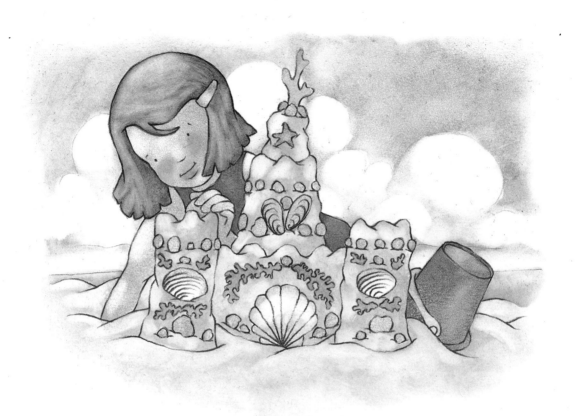

I built a sand castle.

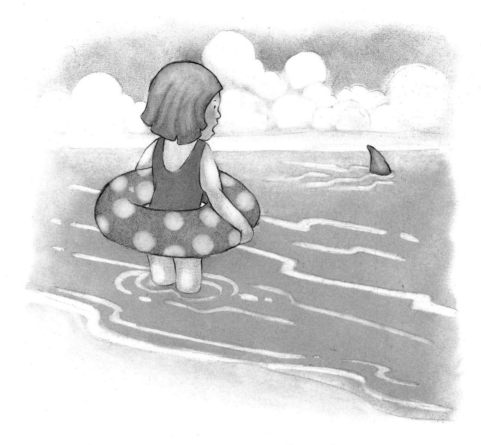

I saw a shark.

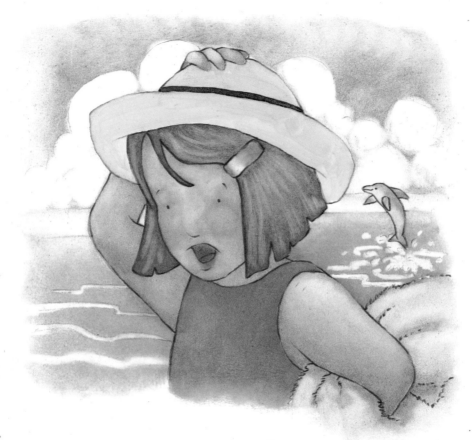

So I left.